19
read a
either a lot of money or a library card.
Cheap paperbacks were available, but their
poor production generally mirrored the quality
between the covers. One weekend that year,
Allen Lane, Managing Director of The Bodley Head,
having spent the weekend visiting Agatha Christie,
found himself on a platform at Exeter station trying to
find something to read for his journey back to London.
He was appalled by the quality of the material he had to
choose from. Everything that Allen Lane achieved from that
day until his death in 1970 was based on a passionate belief
in the existence of 'a vast reading public for *intelligent*
books at a low price'. The result of his momentous vision
was the birth not only of Penguin, but of the 'paperback
revolution'. Quality writing became available for the price of
a packet of cigarettes, literature became a mass medium
for the first time, a nation of book-borrowers became a
nation of book-buyers – and the very concept of book
publishing was changed for ever. Those founding
principles – of quality and value, with an overarching
belief in the fundamental importance of reading –
have guided everything the company has
done since 1935. Sir Allen Lane's
pioneering spirit is still very much alive
at Penguin in 2005. Here's to
the next 70 years!

MORE THAN A BUSINESS

'We decided it was time to end the almost customary half-hearted manner in which cheap editions were produced – as though the only people who could possibly want cheap editions must belong to a lower order of intelligence. We, however, believed in the existence in this country of a vast reading public for intelligent books at a low price, and staked everything on it'
Sir Allen Lane, 1902–1970

'The Penguin Books are splendid value for sixpence, so splendid that if other publishers had any sense they would combine against them and suppress them'
George Orwell

'More than a business ... a national cultural asset'
Guardian

'When you look at the whole Penguin achievement you know that it constitutes, in action, one of the more democratic successes of our recent social history'
Richard Hoggart

King Arthur
in the East Riding

SIMON ARMITAGE

PENGUIN BOOKS

PENGUIN BOOKS

Published by the Penguin Group

Penguin Books Ltd, 80 Strand, London WC2R 0RL, England

Penguin Group (USA) Inc., 375 Hudson Street, New York, New York 10014, USA

Penguin Group (Canada), 10 Alcorn Avenue, Toronto, Ontario, Canada M4V 3B2
(a division of Pearson Penguin Canada Inc.)

Penguin Ireland, 25 St Stephen's Green, Dublin 2, Ireland
(a division of Penguin Books Ltd)

Penguin Group (Australia), 250 Camberwell Road, Camberwell, Victoria 3124,
Australia (a division of Pearson Australia Group Pty Ltd)

Penguin Books India Pvt Ltd, 11 Community Centre,
Panchsheel Park, New Delhi – 110 017, India

Penguin Group (NZ), cnr Airborne and Rosedale Roads, Albany,
Auckland 1310, New Zealand (a division of Pearson New Zealand Ltd)

Penguin Books (South Africa) (Pty) Ltd, 24 Sturdee Avenue,
Rosebank 2196, South Africa

Penguin Books Ltd, Registered Offices: 80 Strand, London WC2R 0RL, England

www.penguin.com

All Points North first published by Viking 1998
Published in Penguin Books 1999
This selection published as a Pocket Penguin 2005

2

Set in 10.5/12.5pt Monotype Dante
Typeset by Palimpsest Book Production Limited,
Polmont, Stirlingshire
Printed in England by Clays Ltd, St Ives plc

Contents

Where You're At

True story. Last winter, three men from a village in West Yorkshire went fishing off the coast near Scarborough, and hauled in an unexploded mine from the Second World War. A crowd gathered to look at the bomb, and a reporter from local television turned up to interview the men on the beach. When the reporter asked one of them if they'd been frightened, he said, 'No, we're alright, us.'

*

I live on the border, between two states. On the one hand, I am who I am, and I know who that person is. It's me, and I can prove it. I've got family and friends who'll vouch for me. I've got a birth certificate to show where I'm from, a passport that says where I've been, and neighbours who know where I live. I've lived here all my life, just about, and I know this place like the back of my hand. I know what I'm doing and I know what it's doing to me. And I know about belonging, and which of the people are my lot – us. We're a mixed bunch, although it's all relative, and one of us is no more mixed and no less relative than the rest. Me. On the other hand, sometimes it's somebody else. Those mixed-up days when it's easier to spot yourself in a crowd than recognize yourself in a mirror. On those occasions, it isn't me doing the rounds, getting about, going here, there and everywhere, but it isn't some stranger either. It's the other person, the second one. It's you.

You live on the border. It's a cultural fault-line, this side of it being the Colne Valley, West Yorkshire, the last set of villages strung out along the trans-Pennine A62. Over the hill on the other side is Saddleworth, Lancashire. Saddleworth used to be in Yorkshire but the Boundary Commission recognized the watershed for what it was. One day a sign appeared at the brow of the hill saying *Oldham Metropolitan Borough* in luminous green letters. The day after that, the sign was obliterated with a shot-gun wound, and a hand-painted board with the word *Saddleworth* was planted in front of it, finished off with a huge white rose. The council took down the offending object but a couple of days later it was back, this time in metal, and the official sign torn up from the soil and left mangled on the hard shoulder. This went on for months until the council gave up or couldn't be bothered. Today, both signs stand next to each other, making whatever lies beyond a kind of no man's land. All we know is that this side is Yorkshire, always was, and on the other side the buses are a different colour. People setting off into Saddleworth for the day talk about 'going over the top', as if they shouldn't necessarily be expected back.

Bulletins arrive in various forms, telling you what you're like, who you are. In the morning it's the *Yorkshire Post*, in the evening it's the *Huddersfield Examiner*. At teatime, it's *Look North* with Mike MacCarthy and the beautiful Sophie Rayworth, or on 'the other side' it's *Calendar*, once the hot-seat of Richard Whiteley, the I Claudius of broadcasting. Most of the stories reported involve animals or murder, or ideally both, and occasionally make the national press. A couple of weeks ago, the *Six O'Clock News* reported that pipistrelle bats from Yorkshire have a different dialect from the same bats just over the border in Lancashire. Under the heading 'Batting for Yorkshire', a scientist explained that the bats not only have a separate vocabulary, but also 'talk' at different frequencies, making it impossible for the two groups to communicate and mix. The bottom line is that Yorkshire bats have deeper voices, and are less chatty. The scientist seemed to feel that this was some extraordinary discovery, but to anyone living around here, it made perfect sense. The first village 'over the top' might only be five miles away, but in terms of dialect and language it might as well be in Cornwall. 'Look', in their part of the world, rhymes with 'fluke' or 'spook'. So docs 'book'. So docs 'cook'. 'Look in the book to see how to cook' becomes a very strange business. If the War of the Roses ever kicks off again, this will be the front line, and anyone crossing the divide will have to keep their traps tightly shut.

Of course, accents are what other people have. Further west, Manchester people try not to open their teeth when they speak, and further still again, Scousers are just putting it on.

Marsden is a village of a few thousand people – why bother counting them when you can see most of them from the top of Scout Head, the horizon that looks like an Indian Chief laid flat on his back. One of your friends had the name of the village and his birth-date tattooed under his heart but didn't show his mother for two years – it's that combination of rough and smooth. Your parents live here, and the last of your grandparents, and your sister and her family live just down the road in Slaithwaite. Somebody once asked your dad how long a person would have to live in Marsden before they were no longer 'comers-in'. Your dad looked him in the eye and said 'Fifty years, and you'll be dead then.'

*

Samuel Laycock was born in Marsden. He was a poet. When he was eleven he had some kind of brain dysfunction and moved to Lancashire, ending up in Blackpool for his troubles, but he's remembered in the village in the shape of an up-ended megalith with a square, metal plate bolted to it. The plate bears a small, embossed image of Laycock from the shoulders up, with his balding head, beard and double-breasted jacket, and the words SAMUEL LAYCOCK, MARSDEN BORN POET. Laycock wrote in Pennine dialect. He was only famous through a handful of towns and villages in the North, but sold thousands of copies of his poems, more than most poets manage to shift throughout the whole country in a lifetime. There's only room for one poet in a village the size of Marsden, which makes Laycock somebody to move past or knock over. The best way to get at him is to take his poems and translate them from whatever version of English he wrote in to whatever version of English you practise yourself. But Laycock died in 1894, so he isn't easily ruffled. He looks out over the bowling green and the tennis court and the bandstand and the flag-pole, his metal face going noticeably greener these last few years – a combination of damp weather and envy.

The Pennine Way comes through Marsden. People who've 'done' the Pennine Way remember Marsden as the place they can't quite remember somewhere near the beginning, or the place they had to get through before they got to the end, somewhere near the end. Marsdeners are known as Cuckoos. They once tried to trap the bird because cuckoos herald the beginning of spring, but to bring a long and not very rewarding narrative to its conclusion, they fucked up. Dimwittedness was the main problem, followed by a poor knowledge of civil-engineering techniques and ignorance of one of the cuckoo's most impressive attributes: the ability to fly. In the next village along the valley, Slaithwaiters are known as Moon Rakers, having tried to drag the reflection of the full moon out of the river. Dimwittedness again played an important part in this legend, though people of that village claim that moon raking was a brilliant and spontaneous alibi given to police when spotted retrieving contraband booze from an under-water hiding place. Slaithwaite, 'Slawitt', is one of the most talked-about, mispronounced place-names in the county, second only, probably, to Penistone.

Marsden has a sheep problem. Last week's *Today's the Day* grand final, hosted by Martyn Lewis on BBC2, showed footage of a village resident impounding a marauding lamb, under an ancient law requiring the shepherd to buy back his stock at market price, or see it sold or eaten. Marsdeners moved closer to their television sets, ready to shout out the name of the village as the correct answer. But the question was about the number of stomachs possessed by that species of creature, and the answer was four.

Colne Valley once had a reputation as a hotbed of radical thought and political activism. It figured strongly in the Luddite uprisings. Enoch Taylor is buried in Marsden, whose looms were pulverized by the hammer of the same name, and William Horsfall was, aptly enough, shot from his horse in Milnsbridge, after saying he'd rather ride up to his saddle girths in blood than give in to the demands of the rabble. Out of the dozens of mills along the valley floor, a handful are still working with wool. The rest are converted into units, full of New Age hippies brewing patchouli oil and making ear-rings out of circuit boards, or moored at the side of the river, rotting away like de-commissioned ocean-liners. Weavers' cottages with their double-glazing look down from the hillsides, like old faces wearing new glasses.

In the 1970s, the Valley fell into a long, pleasant afternoon nap. In their sleep, electors stumbled along to voting booths in junior schools and village halls, and put a cross next to the name of Richard Wainwright, Liberal, who held the seat for donkey's years. He was a good man, and that was all anybody needed to know. On your eighteenth birthday he sent you a signed letter on House of Commons stationery welcoming you to the electoral register, and you sold it to your fifteen-year-old friend for ID in the pubs in town. Then in 1987 the unimaginable happened: Graham Riddick, Conservative, was on his way to Westminster. A Union Jack the size of a tea towel hung limply from the 45-degree flag-pole on Marsden Conservative Club. Some quiet demo-graphic revolution had been taking place, and suddenly there were just enough working-class Tories, middle-class snobs, right-wing farmers, upper-class landowners, Pennine busi-nessmen and comers-in to swing things the other way. It should have been expected. The signs were all there. In Sainsbury's car park, domesticated jeeps and people-carriers outnumbered proper cars three to one.

At the next election, with most Conservative MPs hang-ing on by the width of a credit card, Riddick got in again with an increased majority.

Colne Valley. At junior school you supported Huddersfield Town, 'Town'. You'd been taken to see them by a friend of your dad's, who called jackets 'wind-cheaters' and wore driving gloves in the car. Town had won the First Division

Championship three times in a row sometime back in the Stone Age, so there was history, and therefore hope. But because they were crap, you were allowed another team, Leeds, which was where your mother went shopping if she needed an 'outfit' or where you ended up if you didn't get off the train in Town. It was all very simple, until secondary school, when kids from Saddleworth turned up on funny coloured buses, speaking a strange language, wearing red scarfs tied to their wrists and carrying red plastic holdalls with a silhouette of the devil on the side pocket.

You were thirteen when you first went to Old Trafford. Being a Town fan, you'd never seen fifty thousand people gathered together in one lump, and you'd certainly never seen European football. You'd never been to a floodlit match either, and the teams came on to the pitch like Subbuteo men tipped out on a snooker table. This was in the days before supporting Manchester United became like supporting U2 or the Sony Corporation, in the days when you handed cash over the turnstile and walked on to the terrace.

United were playing Juventus, whose goalie, Dino Zoff, was reckoned to be the best in the world at the time. As he trotted out towards the Stretford End where you were standing, a light ripple of applause ran around the ground, and he lifted his arm and held his index finger in the air, to collect the praise and to confirm his status as the world's number one. That was his big mistake. Suddenly he was staring at tens of thousands of outstretched arms, each one carrying a fist or two fingers, and the insults speared at him needed no translation into Italian. Zoff had fallen for the electric handshake. In another sense, in a split second he'd elevated himself from goalkeeper to God, and the crowd were having none of it. For the rest of the match he was a troubled and lonely figure, stood as far away from the crowd as possible, only coming near to pick the ball out of the net.

The next round was against Ajax, in the days when Ajax was still pronounced like a bathroom cleaner. You were in the Scoreboard End. Before the kick-off, a man behind you leant over the barrier and spat a hot wet blob of bubble gum into your hair. Your friend's dad told you to leave it alone, but you messed with it for ninety minutes, and when you got back, you had to have a bald patch hacked into the top of your head to get rid of the chuddie. At school next day, you got battered for saying where you'd been, and battered again for looking like a medieval monk. You can't remember the score, but the net outcome was a defeat.

You went away to college in Portsmouth for three years at the time when the Fleet was setting out for the South Atlantic, and got glassed in the head in a pub for being from Up North and for looking like a sailor. When you came home at Christmas you got punched for going Down South and for saying Malvinas instead of Falklands. If the stitches in the scalp were a kind of 'keep out', then the black eye was a kind of 'welcome home', and you got both messages loud and clear. A couple of months ago, the Vice-Chancellor of Portsmouth University (as it is now) wrote to you asking 'if you would be willing to accept the confer-ment of the Degree of Doctor of Letters in recognition of your outstanding contribution to the modern poetry movement'. In your dreams, you're congratulated by a professor with a parchment in one hand and a broken Pils bottle behind his back in the other.

*

You worked for the Probation Service in Manchester for six years, driving round estates looking at bruised children, writing reports on smack-heads who were shooting up in their groin, listening to the coppers in the cells under the courthouse singing 'Police release me let me go'. You once rushed a baby to hospital with a suspected cigarette burn on his chest. The doctor examined the baby and said, 'Where?'

'There,' you said.

'Where?' asked the doctor.

'There,' you said, pointing at the bright red mark on the baby's skin.

'That's his nipple,' said the doctor. 'He's got another one on the other side just like it.'

You worked with one lad who got stabbed in the small of his back trying to swipe a bag of heroin from his dealer. He didn't go to hospital till he was shitting out of the hole, three days later. The son of a woman on your caseload died in an incident involving a bathful of scalding water. They took all your files away for inspection, but you'd done everything by the book. The monstrous bird of guilt circled above the town looking for somewhere to strike, but those out in the open kept their nerve when they stood in the cold of its shadow, and those who could offer it a thick skin or a pair of tight lips to home in on kept well under cover, and it flew off over the red-brick houses, robbed of its kill.

You went to a block of flats once to interview an old woman about something or other, and her Alsatian dog followed you through the door and into the front-room. After about half an hour, the dog got up and crapped in the corner, then sat back down by the fire. At first you thought it was none of your business, but eventually you couldn't keep your mouth shut, and asked her why she didn't make her dog go outside. 'It's not my dog,' she said, 'I thought it was yours.' Actually, that story isn't true, but people told it so many times you started to believe it happened to you.

Another woman you worked with had three kids, massive debts and no money. You went round to her house one day and there was a huge Rottweiler bitch in the kitchen, eating a bucket of food.

'What have you got that for?' you asked the woman.

'Ten quid,' she said.

On another visit the dog wouldn't stop growling at you. 'Don't worry,' the woman said. 'It's because you're drinking out of her cup.' That story isn't true either.

Before you parted company with the Probation Service, you were working as the Bail Intervention Officer at Oldham Magistrates' Court. Every day was different, every day was the same. Every morning at about seven o'clock, you turned up at the police station and, if you remembered the passwords and key-codes, made your way along a concrete tunnel, up a flight of stairs, and emerged in the holding cells under the courtroom. The desk sergeant, if he was in a good mood, gave you a list of the men and women arrested overnight, along with a few details of the offences. If he'd got out of bed on the wrong side, or hadn't been asked to do overtime at Old Trafford for the big match on Saturday, you sat there like a lemon until one of the other officers finished his coffee and threw a bunch of papers at you.

The holding area was a few desks and telephones, iron gates at either end of a long corridor, half a dozen cells to either side, and a glass interview room in the middle, known as the goldfish bowl. Usually, there were five or six men in each cell, in various stages of alertness, ranging from the comatose drunk to the manic junkie. They'd shout through the narrow grille in the metal door until one of the officers put down the newspaper, hauled himself off his chair and strolled over to the cell, his Doc Martens squeaking on the lino floor.

'I'll need a piss, Boss.'

'You've had a piss. Tie a knot in it.'

'Give us a spark, Boss.'

A cigarette comes poking out through the mesh. The officer holds a lighted match just out of reach. 'Say "please".'

'Don't be a cunt, Boss. Give us a spark.'

The officer might light the cigarette, or he might not.

'Come on, Boss, I need a piss.'

If he can be bothered the officer opens the door with one of the keys hanging from his belt-loop, and a cloud of Old Holborn billows into the corridor. Bodies come to light at the back of the room: asleep, smoking, doing press-ups, staring, yawning. Someone emerges and the officer marches him to the toilet, waiting outside to walk him back again.

'Come on, get on with it. If you shake it more than twice you're having a wank.'

'Boss, there's no paper.'

'So use your sleeve.'

'Boss, will I get bail, will I?'

'You'll go to hell if it's up to me, but I'm sure this nice gentleman from the Probation Service might sort you out a five-star hotel for a few weeks.'

*

It was the job of the nice man from the Probation Service to present 'positive, factual, and verified' information to the court that might lead to an offender being bailed to a second appearance, rather than held in custody. At least, that was the written-down version. In reality, he tried to remind the bench that bail was a right, not a privilege, and wanted to impress on them the idea that a shoplifter from Glodwick with a house and a family is more likely to come back to court to face the punishment than flee to a luxury villa in Marbella, beyond the grasp of British justice.

In the goldfish bowl, you ran through a standard list of questions as they called the bodies out of the cells, one at a time. For most of them, you were the first person they'd seen since being nabbed, and after a year or so you reckoned you could fit the character to the crime without asking.

Puke or blood down the front of his shirt, wanting to know the time: Drunk and Disorderly.

Calm and quiet, saying nothing without speaking to a solicitor: Possession with Intent to Supply.

Asking you to phone up and tell her he's sorry: Actual Bodily Harm.

Seventeen, wedge haircut, trainers: Taking without Owner's Consent.

Track marks up the arm, saying that she needs the kids taking to her mother's: Shoplifting.

Eyes on stalks, a muscle throbbing at the back of the jaw, reeling off improbabilities one after another: Illegal Possession of a Controlled Substance.

Alert, mindful, innocent: Indecent Assault.

Terrified, short of breath: Manslaughter.

Silent, heavy, sad: Murder.

Angry, flabbergasted, indignant: Guilty.

Bewildered, tearful, compliant: Guilty.

Stereotypes – a stupid game to play, but there was satisfaction in getting it right and satisfaction in getting it wrong. In any event, it wasn't as if you were judging them by the distance between their eyes. The magistrates did that. Your job was to drive round to a house, knock on a door and wait for someone to come downstairs or open a bedroom window, usually a wife or a mother in a nightdress.

YOU: 'Mrs So-and-so?'

HER: 'Who wants to know?'

YOU: 'Probation.'

HER: 'What's he done this time?'

YOU: 'Nicked a car.'

HER: 'What do you want me to do about it?'

YOU: 'Is this his address?'

HER: 'I should hope so, he lives here.'

YOU: 'Is he working?'

HER: 'Yes, he's Managing Director of ICI.'

YOU: 'OK, thanks.'

HER: 'What time's he up in court?'

YOU: 'Sometime after ten.'

HER: 'Hang on a minute, I'll come with you.'

There was no natural light in the holding area, only fluorescent strips, and the police worked eight- or nine-hour shifts. They handcuffed prisoners to their own wrists, walked them through the iron gates and upstairs into the courtroom, stood with them in the dock, then dragged them back down to the cells to be carted off to Strangeways. They were known as the pit ponies.

*

Driving back to West Yorkshire through the cutting every night was a way of shutting the door behind you, watching the *Oldham Metropolitan Borough* sign disappear in the rear-view mirror. Always work away from home. Don't bring dirt to your own doorstep. Always set off to the west in a morning and come back to the east at night – that way you keep the sun out of your eyes. Always live where the rivers run from left to right, like writing.

Your front door opens out on to some of the most empty and dangerous countryside in Britain. Hundreds of square miles of saturated earth and rotting peat, a kind of spongy version of the sea. When you were a kid you walked across the moors looking for dead bodies, but found tractor tyres instead, or fridge-freezers, or crash helmets, miles from anything or anywhere. The only other thing to do was to break into the air shafts above the railway tunnel and drop stones on to the Liverpool train.

At the same time as being remote and away from it all, you're only an hour away from Sheffield, Leeds, Bradford or Manchester, and only one hour forty-three minutes from London on the Electrified East Coast Line, the rail route that's turned Wakefield and Doncaster into commuter towns.

At least, it was one hour forty-three minutes the last time you looked, but the people who own the line this week have probably got together with the people who own the rolling stock, who might have spoken to the cartel who've just bought the signalling system, who could quite possibly have made contact with the catering company and the maintenance contractors, and another couple of minutes might have been sliced off the travelling time. Not that you can moan about covering two hundred miles in less than an hour and three-quarters, but you do get the feeling that a bit more introspection rather than the odd bit of interaction might make things even quicker, and certainly a lot less complicated. And if you need information on connections to trans-Pennine services at this end (those trains that look like buses, with the brake system linked to the door mechanism so that the train won't move if the door isn't water-tight) or one of the lines hooking into London when you get there – tough.

The Electrified East Coast Line is the main artery in a rail network suffering from poor circulation and amputation. At the auction, this was the working part that the latter-day body-snatchers wanted to bid for. The swankiest trains in the country, recently painted a sinister, nuclear-waste-carrying blue, glide up and down between London and Edinburgh, collecting passengers at certain mainline stations, sweeping through others at the speed of thought, leaving a vacuum behind, followed by a hurricane. It's said that Yorkshire prostitutes travel to London on these trains for a week's work in the Big Smoke, and make enough in the toilets on the way down to pay for the ticket. Which particular ticket they prefer hasn't been recorded, because purchasing one is not an easy business given the variety of choice, including Apex, Daypex, SuperAdvance, SuperSaver, Saver, and Standard. A basic tip here is not to head south from these parts before ten o'clock in the morning, or you're looking at a hundred pounds. That is unless you've bought your ticket in London and you're travelling on the return portion, which is what the businessmen and women of Yorkshire do, in which case you can save yourself or your company fifty quid. The highest fares are for the ignorant and those poor souls who go to the capital less than once a month.

There are also rules against travelling on Fridays and travelling north at teatime, just in case you'd wondered about coming home for the weekend. Then there's the question of class. The trains running north-south usually arrive with the First-Class carriages to the front and the Standard-Class to the rear, with a buffet car in the middle as a border point. The smoking carriages are located at the very back – presumably towed on a length of rope. Everyone in Britain knows you can never change your class, but not everyone knows that by taking breakfast in the First-Class restaurant car at Newark, perhaps, or maybe Grantham, you can just about spin out the last corner of toast and the last thimble of marmalade to Welwyn Garden City, by which time you're safe. Breakfast does cost £12.50, and you will be offered black pudding, but it's cheaper than buying the correct ticket, and creates a certain amount of excitement, given that the view out of the window, for most of the way, is Lincolnshire.

There is another category of class, however, which goes under the name of Silver Standard, made up of one or two carriages forming a buffer zone between First and Standard. For a few pounds more than the cheapest fare, you can separate yourself from your fellow commoners and be served with bottomless coffee from Wakefield Westgate to King's Cross. You'll also be furnished with a handkerchief-sized Silver Standard cloth, draped over the headrest, to absorb the sweat or grease from the back of your head and, more importantly, protect the back of your head from the sweat and the grease of previous passengers. On the downside, Silver Standard is always full, because the merchants of the North are falling over each other to distinguish themselves from their kith and kin, especially if it only costs a couple of sovs. In their eighty-twenty suits and Crimplene skirts, the whole carriage humming with static electricity and perspiration, they look down their noses and over the top of their complimentary *Daily Telegraphs* at those pitiful travellers having to fetch their own rust-coloured tea and Sandwich of the Month from the buffet. Back down the line in the cattle trucks, the SuperSavers spread their magazines and books over the tables and put their feet up on the seat opposite.

You live just to the left of where the upright of one great communication corridor slashes the crossbar of another, a good place for going away from and coming back to, a good place for getting the gist. The North, where the M1 does its emergency stop, and away over the back of the hill is the M62, gouged into the moorland and completely out of its element. At one point, the carriageways separate to pass each side of a farm, and a farmer brings his cows for milking at dusk through a subway, into his central reservation. Thousands of tons of steel pass any given point every minute of the day, but when the winter brings the motorway to a frozen standstill, convoys are snuffed out by the snow in less than an hour, and vehicles are excavated weeks later like woolly mammoths out of the tundra. The M62, like a belt drawn tightly across the waistline of Britain, with the buckle somewhere near Leeds.

From the observation suite of Emley Moor Mast, not much short of a thousand feet of fluted concrete with a hypodermic aerial on top, just south of Huddersfield, you can see both coasts. Or you could do, if you were allowed up it and the weather was clear, which you aren't, and even if you were, it wouldn't be. From Castle Hill, the other local landmark, the next highest ground going east are the Ural Mountains in Russia, and you can't see them either.

It's the middle distance really, but you call it the North. The North, where England tucks its shirt in its underpants. It's not all to do with Peter Snow's election map being mainly blue at the bottom and completely red at the top, although that comes into it. And it's more complicated than women wearing rollers and aprons, scrubbing the front step and boil-washing their husbands' shirts, and their husbands pissing in the sink if the wife's on the toilet, and their daughters in snow-washed supermarket jeans and crop-tops eating baked beans straight from the can, and their arm-wrestling sons farting in the one-minute silence at Hillsborough and turning over the mobile Ultra-Burger hot-dog stand after a night on the sauce, although that comes into it as well. The North can also be Lancashire, which is really the North-West, and it can also be Northumberland, which is the North-East, and sometimes it's Humberside, which is the Netherlands, and it can be Cumbria, which is the Lake District, and therefore Scotland. But right here is the North, with its gods and its devils; where Jarvis Cocker meets Geoffrey Boycott, where Emily Brontë meets David Batty, where Ted Hughes meets Darren Gough, where David Hockney meets Peter Sutcliffe, where Brian Glover meets Henry Moore, and where Bernard Ingham meets Prince Naseem Hamed, or at least if there's any justice he does.

In one sense, it's neither here nor there; land with a line drawn around it for no particular reason, too far-flung to give a single name, too divided into layers and quarters and stripes to think of as whole, too many claims on it to call your own.

But in another sense, it's where you're at, the big piece of the jigsaw. The place between the shoreline and the ridge, between the middle and the rest. The place between the stainless-steel Minotaur keeping guard over Meadowhall, and the kitchen sink; between the Brick Man of Holbeck, who never was, and the Cowthorpe Oak, the country's oldest living thing, which is no more. The place between the fifty-foot drifts of '47, and last year's reservoirs backed into dust-bowls and craters of the moon; between cotton-grass bleaching its hair on White Moss, and a bird's-eye view of the Humber Bridge. Between the rocking stone at Brandreth Crags and the last pebble on Spurn Point; between the red deer and the pygmy shrew; between the four-lane stretch from Junction 25 to Ainley Top, and the Lyke Wake Walk. The place between the male-voice choir, and the Western Terrace singing this year's chant on the first day of the Headingley Test; the Goldcrest, and the bones of elephants and big cats in Kirkdale cave; the secret Lady's Slipper orchid, and the burning of the saints; Good Friday's Pace Egg Play, and open season on 1st April. The place between Kilnsea and Lower Bentham, Totley and Staithes; between Bangladesh and Bradford Interchange; between the flea with its teeth in anything that moves, and the magpie with its charm; Halifax PLC, and the worst busker in Leeds without a penny to scratch his arse. Between the fly who'll drink with anyone, and the side of bacon – better when hung; between those lying dead in their graves like cargo lost from the shipwreck of Heptonstall Church, and those coming back from the sea with their lives into Grimsby and Hull; between the aerials and masts decoding babble and gibberish out of the air, and the deep, cathedral quiet of Gaping Gill, three hundred feet below ground; between the rocks in the cairns on the tops of the hills, and the hard places down in the seven cities and hundred towns.

It's halfway to heaven, they reckon, here in the county with more acres than letters in the Bible. It's the distance between, the difference of this from the next, one from another. And you, you live on the border.

*

Late News: Last week, the word *Lancashire* was daubed in red paint across the Saddleworth sign and its white rose. It isn't clear if the action was taken by people on this side of the hill who've turned against their former county-folk, or people from the far side, who've thrown in the towel.

King Arthur in the East Riding

> And if they go away from home, their reason is equally
> cogent: 'What does it signify how we dress here, where
> nobody knows us?'
> – Mrs Gaskell, *Cranford*

We must look like a pretty odd collection of people, the
ninety of us gathered by the lych-gate with suitcases and
bags at half-nine on a Saturday morning. One man cracks
open a can of beer and his wife shakes her head in despair.
A woman in a spangly gold blouse and leggings pours tea
from a flask and offers the cup round. A couple come out
of a house across the road and join the rest of us, talking
about the weather and looking at our watches. When the
two coaches arrive, we load the bags and cases into the
big black cave of each boot, and the drivers in their short-
sleeved white shirts with black epaulettes share a cigarette,
one of them flicking the smouldering dimp into the river.
Someone scurries about with a clipboard ticking off names
from a list: Muskett, Haig, Carter, Howarth, Norcliffe,
Armitage, Byrom, Lodge, Hall, Hoyle, Dyson, Schorthorn,
Whitehead, Kewley – we couldn't really be from anywhere
else other than West Yorkshire.

The wagon turns up, full to the back with props, costumes
and scenery, and the driver sounds the horn a couple of times
making a noise like an American freight train, leading the
convoy up Peel Street and out of the village.

We're a mixed bunch, there's no doubt about that, with

very different ideas about what to wear for a weekend in Bridlington at the end of April. For some people it's jeans, trainers and a T-shirt, for others it's a heavy woollen suit with braces and brogues, and for those of us who've spent any time on Yorkshire's east coast, it's a thick jumper with a waterproof coat in reserve. Most of us talk louder than we need to about which guesthouse we're staying in, how we're going to kill time before the evening, whether or not we've remembered to pack everything we need. The coach stops a couple more times along the main road to pick up the handful of people who don't actually live in the village, then on into Huddersfield. Past the derelict façade of Ivanhoe's nightclub where the Sex Pistols played their last British gig – the gig that you always say you went to, but didn't. Past the McAlpine Stadium, Huddersfield Town's relocated ground looking like a blue and white lunar module – enough of a stadium to host the likes of REM and Oasis last year, and some half-decent football matches as well. Past the scrapyard where Peter Sutcliffe bought his false number-plates, and then we're chugging up the slip road and on to the motorway.

The man in front of me studies the racing pages of the *Yorkshire Post*. The man in front of him shouts out crossword clues from the *Guardian*. The man in front of him can't wait a minute longer, and unpacks a steaming bacon butty from a parcel of silver foil. In front of him, two men go through a script together, rehearsing lines.

'I'd give you a peck on the cheek, but I've got scruples.'

'Don't worry, Lancelot, I've already had them.'

'I shall seal our love with a kiss.'

'I'm hoping we can seal it a lot tighter than that!'

'Guinevere, I love you. I shall kiss you on the lips or bust.'

'Well make your mind up!'

And so on. On the M62 the coaches and the wagon overtake each other, which brings about a variety of hand signals and gestures, ranging from a royal wave to an up-and-down movement of the thumb and index finger in the shape of a circle, mainly between the men towards the back end of each coach. The wagon driver pomps the horn again as we overtake him up the hill out of Brighouse. Further along, we pass two double-deckers doing fifty on the inside lane, the first one full of Asian women sitting downstairs, the second full of Asian men sitting upstairs, both buses painted orange and turquoise. We wave, and they wave back. 'Wedding job,' someone says, and everyone agrees.

Further east, on the section of the motorway that becomes straight and quiet like a runway, we turn off at the Goole exit along a road running between two fields of sugar beet, before pulling on to the gravel forecourt of a truck stop, the bus bottoming on the uneven surface of pot-holes and puddles.

'Greasy Spoon,' somebody moans.

'It's a road-house,' his wife corrects him. 'I'll have tea and an orange Kit-Kat.'

Whatever the Redbeck Café is or isn't, the six or seven customers inside are slightly bemused when we all pile in, and a man in an orange Railtrack diddy-jacket puts on his glasses to watch us forming an orderly but noisy queue between the formica tables and the video games. A lorry driver pumps money into a slot-machine in the far corner that plays *The Star Spangled Banner* every time it spits out a ten-pence piece. A couple with two children smoke without speaking to each other, while their kids lick their fingers and draw on the table with ash from the ashtray. In our party, the hungriest push to the front to order the breakfast special, a slimy mound of bacon, eggs, mushrooms, sausage, beans, fried bread and tomatoes, covered over with a helping of chips. £2.30. The rest of us stand for twenty minutes, soaking up the cigarette smoke and the hot fat in the air, reading the 'Missing, Can-U-Help' posters of long-lost teenagers and watching Monster Truck Racing on the telly bolted to the wall. You're sent by some of the women to check out the toilets, and walk down a long corridor with battered shower units to the left with wooden pallets on the floor to stand on. You're expecting the loos at the far end to be slarted with the shit of a thousand lorry-driving arses, but they're clean and shiny, with dozens of toilet rolls stashed behind the flush-pipe like rounds of ammunition. You give the thumbs up, and the women set off down the dark corridor towards the cubicles, in pairs.

Most people have taken their drinks outside and are sitting on a concrete wall with the sun just beginning to break through. A twelve-wheeler spins out of the car park throwing up a small grey cloud of dust, and some of the men look on admiringly. A woman feeds the last bit of a sausage sandwich to a dog through a half-opened car window, and shrieks when it wolfs down the paper plate as well. Your mum comes outside with red cheeks and tears rolling down her face. 'Swallowed a crumb,' she manages to croak, and someone slaps her hard between the shoulder-blades until she coughs it out. Your dad lights his pipe and blows the smoke through his teeth with his head back, looking at the sky. Then he turns around and sees you watching him, and winks. You nod your head. Then the wagon driver gives one long pull on the horn, like the klaxon at the end of a Rugby League match, and we climb back on the buses, some people wiping the grease from their lips on the back of their hands, some people spilling coffee from styrofoam cups as we wobble out of the car park on to the road. The next twenty or thirty miles are a steady cruise between fields of potatoes with scarecrows crucified left, right and centre, and past hundreds of pigs, sunning themselves outside their own cut-down Anderson shelters.

As we get near the edge of town, there's growing excitement on the coach. People stand up to get a better view, even though there's nothing to see. Nearly everyone in West Yorkshire has been to 'Brid' on holiday at some time in their life, just like nearly everyone in Lancashire has been to Blackpool, and there's a great deal of this-is-where-so-and-so-happened or isn't-that-where-what's-his-face-did-such-and-such, before we turn off the High Street into avenues where every house has a B&B sign outside and a 'Vacancies' notice in the window.

At the front of the bus, someone pipes up, 'This is like going to Wembley,' which is a nice idea but not really a fair comparison. Amateur footballers probably dream of the twin towers every night, but nobody at Pule Side Working Men's Club ever had any real desire to perform their all-male panto anywhere other than the village hall. When the Northern Operatic and Dramatic Association asked us to take the production to their annual conference, at the thousand-seater Spa Theatre, it was such a pie-in-the-sky and off-the-wall and out-of-the-blue idea that nobody really knew what it was we'd agreed to. But that was six months ago, and today's the day, and tonight's the night, and it's a big deal. The bus draws up alongside four landladies having a chin-wag on the pavement; we're taken off to our guesthouses, all within fifty yards and facing each other. There are more hand signals and gestures across the street from those of us with rooms at the front.

Although Bridlington's gone the way of most seaside towns during the last twenty years, it still has its self-respect. It might be one of England's deteriorating coastal resorts, but it also has the feel of a place where people live and work, even if it isn't clear what they do. We walk through what might well be the rough end of town, past a butcher's with meat going grey in the window, past half a dozen charity shops selling socks from plastic dustbins at £3.99 for five pairs, and another with pac-a-macs, acrylic 'ganseys' and brown polyester 'slacks' hung up on the outside of the window. In the town centre, four of us call at an ice-cream parlour for a knickerbocker glory, something you were never allowed when you came here on holiday. Segments of tinned fruit sink like slugs to the bottom of a glass chalice where molten ice-cream curdles with half an inch of raspberry-coloured chemicals. It's disgusting, and we end up catapulting pineapple chunks at each other with the long-handled spoons. We're also disappointed to see that it isn't even the most expensive item, and that for another thirty pence we could have gone the whole hog with an ice-cream sundae, any flavour.

Everyone's split up now, and we keep bumping into various branches of the tribe along the prom and on the harbour. Muskett goes past with a fried haddock hanging from his mouth, unable to speak. The Whitehead sisters have just bought two Supa-Soaka pump-action water pistols for their kids, and grin as they go by sharing the ear-plugs of the same Walkman, mouthing the words of the same song.

You're gawping into a shop, 'Hilda's', that has twelve pairs of enormous white knickers laid out in the window without price or explanation, when your mum taps you on the back. 'Enjoying yourself?'

'Yeah. Where's Dad?'

She points in the direction of the Spa. 'He's on pins. He's gone for a snoop.'

I can see him walking along the front towards the theatre, pipe smoke curling over his shoulder.

'You know what he's like,' she says. 'See you later.'

She marches off up the street to join him, and you watch him pointing out some feature on the big grey building in front of them with the glass cupola. They're looking at the zipper sign on the side of the theatre, with the moving message advertising tonight's performance in electric-red letters.

If he is more nervous than the rest of us, then he's probably got every right to be. For one thing, he wrote the pantomime, and for another, he's the producer. No matter how much any one else is involved, it's all down to him in the end. Not only that, he's putting himself on the line in front of his friends and colleagues from the strange world of amateur dramatics, and putting his faith in a bunch of blokes whose common bond has nothing to do with acting or singing and everything to do with the club where they go drinking. He's slapped a 'no getting pissed' order on the cast, but given that we don't go on stage till midnight, the chances of it holding are pretty non-existent. He walks on towards the theatre with my mum, and another puff of tobacco smoke rises up into the ether.

*

To pass the time, we walk along the cliff path to Sewerby, the better end of Bridlington, despite what the first two syllables of its name might suggest. We pay for a game of crown green bowls, but because our footwear is 'too clumpy' we're invited to wear a pair of overshoes – rubber heels with straps, like the back half of a black sandal, or something given to a child with one leg shorter than the other. The green-keeper fishes them out of a big cardboard box that looks as if it might have gas masks in the bottom as well. We waddle around on the green for an hour in our surgical appliances, taking great divots out of the turf every time we trip up, then wander back towards the town, past the profoundly sad or blissfully contented donkeys carrying children backwards and forwards along the cliff-top for fifty pence a go.

Having dragged its heels all afternoon, the day suddenly begins picking up pace, gaining momentum towards midnight. At six o'clock we're eating a curry in Bridlington's best Indian restaurant. Someone's written 'Very fantastic' in the visitors' book. Five minutes later, at seven o'clock, we're striding down North Marine Drive in black jackets and white shirts, five of us, like the beginning of *Reservoir Dogs*. Nobody says so, but somebody whistles the tune. Ten more seconds and it's half-eight, and we're sitting in the back five rows of the stalls watching the 'other' show, Whitby Operatics singing a London Medley in cod cock-ney accents, followed by a selection of songs and routines from *Oklahoma* to *Oliver*, with no apparent connection. During the wedding scene from *Fiddler on the Roof*, the groom's father sings the line 'When did he get to be so tall?' and looks proudly towards his son, who just happens to be the smallest man on the stage by a good six inches.

Half the people in the audience implode with convulsions of suppressed laughter, and the other half laugh out loud. Fortunately, the man himself sees the funny side of it, and even from where we're sitting we can see that he's smiling. We're generous with our applause because we know that in three hours' time they'll be part of the audience listening to us, but privately we're glad it's nothing better than pretty good. You can hear your dad thinking, 'It's not a competition, but we can win it.'

During the half an hour it takes Whitby to clear the stage and dressing-rooms, we go for a drink in the ballroom, and find out there's been a bit of 'afters' between some of our contingent in the balcony and a man who whooped and wolf-whistled and made other animal noises during the concert. He's been asked politely at least three times, apparently, but not to any effect, and as a consequence, somebody has followed him into the toilets to 'have a word'. No one asks which particular word it is, but when our man comes back to the bar readjusting his tie and straightening his cuffs, that's the end of the matter.

Eventually, finally, we're allowed backstage, and clamber up through the orchestra pit and look out into the empty auditorium. It might not be the Albert Hall, but it makes Marsden Parochial Hall look like a doll's house. Somebody shouts, 'Hello,' and the word disappears into the gloom beyond the front of the balcony. Spotlights clunk into action somewhere up in the gods, blinding us all for a minute. Just when we're on the verge of wondering what the hell we're doing, doors swing open at the side of the stage and the wagon backs up to the entrance. For the next half an hour we haul boxes and crates and cases and bags into the wings, stretchering rails of clothes to far-away dressing-rooms, hooking curtains and batons to cables and ropes that hoik them upwards into the rafters, marking the floor with chalk and gaffer-tape, then dragging great blocks of scenery juddering into position. Green, yellow and purple lights flood the stage, and the lighting-crew strut around wearing microphone headsets, like air-traffic controllers.

Dad stands in front of the stage, about five rows back, bawling orders at everyone and checking his watch. At about half-eleven, when it looks like we might have time for a bit of a rehearsal, there's a technical hitch, and we have to make do with singing a couple of songs and speeding through a few pages of dialogue. At quarter to twelve, from behind the closed curtain, we can hear the chattering and chunnering of a thousand am-dram snobs from all over the North – big women in glittery backless dresses and mock-croc stilettos, small cigar-smoking men in white tuxedos with long-service medals pinned to their breast pockets – all fingering the makeshift programme that one of us slipped through the office photocopier during a fire alarm.

At five to twelve, most of us are lined up in a corridor outside the make-up room, not saying much. King Arthur blots his lipstick on a napkin, and Merlin clamps his stick-on beard to his chin. One of the fairies asks one of the knights to do up his dress at the back, and another fairy stuffs a third pair of socks into his bra. A man who has only ever been seen with a pint glass in his hand takes a long slug from a bottle of mineral water. A bottle of Johnny Walker Black Label gets passed around, but no one has more than a toothful. Over the intercom we can hear the audience applauding the orchestra – two pianists and the village barber on drums – then a few seconds' pause before the first bars of the overture. Dad calls us all on to stage as if he's about to give a team talk or make some big speech, but he just says 'Enjoy it,' and disappears. We line up across the stage in darkness, and then silence, and stare at the thick red curtain in front of our faces, until it flies open.

From out there it must look very weird, even for a pantomime. We range in height from five-foot-nothing to six-foot-five. In age, from fourteen to sixty-odd. In weight, probably from around eight stone, soaking wet, to something approaching twenty, with those at the top end carrying a lot of it just above the belt. Maybe this wouldn't be so unusual if all the various bodies weren't squeezed into tights, leggings, tutus, tabards, smocks and capes, and if the faces and heads above them weren't caked in panstick and crowned with wigs, smurf hats or tiaras. No one's ever asked why it's an all-male performance, which is just as well because nobody really knows, and it must be obvious by the time we've barked through the first number that no one's expecting red roses at the stage door, or a recording contract, or an audition in the West End.

There's a split second at the end of the song when nothing happens, a hard silence, in which every one of us on stage must wonder if the audience have taken it the wrong way, if they haven't 'approved', if they haven't 'got it'. But it is only a split second, and then an avalanche of clattering applause follows us off the stage and into the dressing-room, to jump into the next robe or frock or chain-mail tank-top and get back out under the lights.

Enjoy it. And we do. From when Arthur yanks the plywood sword from the papier mâché stone to an hour later when, in an unexpected twist to the legend of Camelot, Merlin plugs him with a Second World War revolver, turning to the audience and saying 'Well, he wasn't up to the job.'

During the finale, the stage staff sidle on to stage, followed by your dad in a dinner jacket and bow tie. Even through the darkness at the back of the hall, it's possible to see everybody in the balcony stood up and cheering, waving their programmes, and he stands with his hands behind his back, leaning forward into the applause as if it were sunlight on his face.

The curtains sweep across, and that's it. In one of the dressing-rooms there's a scrum for the only bar of soap as thirty of us try to wash in one bowl of lukewarm water, like hippos round the last muddy puddle at the water hole, and in five minutes we're striding back up the promenade, ready for a drink. It's two in the morning.

No one can really remember how it went, but it doesn't matter, because in the private bar of the Mon Fort Hotel we go through the whole damn thing again, song by song, eighty or ninety of us now, plus three or four bewildered residents in the corner, smiling nervously. At one stage, a drunk in a lumberjack jacket comes in from the street and wanders over to the buffet table, and has to be given 'the Scarborough warning'. I don't know what the Scarborough warning is, exactly; a lot of the men have just had their fiftieth birthdays, which makes them part of the baby-boom generation, and every now and again they fall into a kind of armed-forces lingo which probably came from their fathers. Whatever it is, it works, and the lumberjack returns to his seat outside on the pavement, staring at the seafood vol-au-vents and tandoori chicken drumsticks through one of the bottom panes in the bay window.

*

Nights like these never end. Whatever time you decide to pack it in, there's always somebody at the bar buying another round, and always somebody at breakfast saying how the landlord went to bed and told everybody to put their money in the till. It's more a question of selecting your own personal point of exit – like jumping off a merry-go-round that never stops – and just before the sun comes up, half a dozen of us spill out on to the road and amble back to the B&B through a cold sea-fret, ready for the end of the day. Four hours later, there's a full English breakfast for those who can manage one, and tea and dry toast for those who can't, served in a mock Tudor dining-room which also incorporates a Scottish theme, including a tartan carpet, a St Andrews golf-ball cruet set, a framed photograph of a Highland Terrier wearing a sporran round its neck, and a set of bagpipes nailed to the wall above the bar like a Loch Ness octopus. Somebody rattles paracetamol like dice in a tumbler, and everybody wants one. Eventually we all stumble out of the guesthouse into the sunshine, dragging suitcases and bags on to the pavement, and the coaches arrive. Some of the party from the B&B across the road have started drinking again – either that, or they never stopped – and we fill the street, pointing at one another and laughing, saying how great it was, going on about it.

Riding home, we loll about on the back seat telling stories about school. How Mrs Dyson made Terry Pamment piss his britches by saying, 'You *can* go to the toilet, but you *may* not.' How Jumbo Ellis and his mates broke into the school, and Ellis got stuck in the window, trapping them all inside like a cork.

'He was ginormous,' says someone.

'He's dead,' says someone else.

How a fifth-former threw half a dozen hens into the school one night, followed by a fox.

'That true?'

'Nope,' says the person telling the story.

All the way down the bus, people fall asleep against the windows, their faces and hair squashed flat, leaving big greasy smudges on the glass. We arrive at the church gates, tired and a little bit sunburnt, telling each other we can't decide if it feels like a lifetime ago or no time at all. The old people in the flats across the road stare out of their windows at us, wondering if it was this morning when they saw us loading suitcases into the back of the bus, or possibly yesterday, or maybe the week before last. Everyone sets off walking home, slowly, traces of lipstick still colouring their mouths, stubble growing out through a hint of rouge, mascara hiding the sleep in their eyes.

The Tyre

One touch of nature makes the whole world kin,
That all with one consent praise new-born gawds,
Though they are made and moulded of things past
– Shakespeare, *Troilus and Cressida*

The human heart is like Indian rubber
– Anne Brontë, *Agnes Grey*

Lo, all our pomp of yesterday
Is one with Nineveh and Tyre!
– Kipling, 'Recessional'

You've just finished writing a poem about a tyre. In the first half of the poem, you remember finding a tractor tyre on the moor behind your parents' house, then rolling it down into the village with four or five friends, to burn on Bonfire Night. Somewhere during the last year or so, you've begun to think of your upbringing as supernatural in some way, a notion based mainly on experiences like this one with the tyre, experiences involving some element of exploration or expedition, and quite often ending in mystery or alchemy. In a similar incident, you and your friends made lead ingots by melting down metal stripped from rooftops and windows, having discovered all the necessary tackle buried in the earth under the mill. Who'd left it there?

*

It wasn't unusual to go wandering off over the hills, just as it wasn't unusual to find things in the middle of nowhere without any reasonable explanation. A bag of golf balls on one occasion, a pram, the bottom half of a turquoise bikini, and so on. In the case of the tyre, we must have tripped right over it, because it was sewn to the earth with tuft-grass and rushes, and the stitching had to be unpicked before we could prize it out of the peat and lift it up.

Growing up plays tricks with the brain, especially where weights and measures are concerned, and if in the end the tyre was actually the spare wheel from a Morris Minor, then so be it. But at the time it was massive; thick-skinned, hardly manageable, a huge monster of a thing, staggering blind drunk across the moor as we rolled it, using the diagonal wedges of its tread as handles.

You're more or less certain that the past, as some poets have already said, is a writer's only reserve. Almost all poems are the products of memory and recollection, as if the process of writing were an effort to recombine with that semi-conscious, half-innocent state of childhood, as if all poems were statements of loss. It's the same lamenting over the past that leads to so much anthropomorphism in poetry, and the sampling of inanimate objects for their human impressions to return to that dream-like country of 'before'. Having come too far to go back, we appeal to the super-conscious to win out over the everyday and the commonplace, to bring about some momentary flash of reconnection. Words are the conductors.

You're also thinking here about the way that very small children don't distinguish between the natural and the unnatural, the way that if a toy train chugged across the carpet under its own steam in front of a child, the laws of the universe wouldn't suddenly come into question. Once you were babysitting for a neighbour, and their little boy wouldn't go to sleep, and you could hear him fidgeting and grunting through the home-made intercom between the bedroom and downstairs. After a couple of hours, you flicked the switch on the tannoy and said, 'Go to sleep,' then flicked back in time to hear him saying to the loud-speaker, 'You shut up, Mr Box.' Animals have the same capabilities. Most people interpret this as the inability to determine between fact and fiction, as we grown-ups understand it.

In the second part of the poem, you describe what happened when the tyre reached the road. The village is down in the bottom of a geographical bowl, with all roads descending into it at a steep angle. This particular road is steeper than most, and straighter, and there came a point at which the tyre gained an unstoppable and terrible momentum. However much we tried to slow it down or tried to wobble it to the ground with rugby tackles and Kung-Fu kicks, it didn't even flinch, and carried on pick-ing up speed towards the junction with the main road across the Pennines. At one stage, it even mounted the banking to turn a right-hand bend, then crossed the A62 between two wagons going at sixty miles an hour in oppo-site directions. You sometimes wonder if the two drivers ever jump from their sleep as a hundredweight of black rubber passes in front of the windscreen.

After the junction, the tyre careered on into the centre of the village, and we lost sight of it as it followed the camber of the street and turned to the left by the grave-yard. Out of breath, with our hearts in our mouths and our hands black with the evidence, we entered the world of houses and shops, expecting broken glass and buckled metal at least, or at worst, the swatted fly of an upturned pram, with its wheels spinning in mid-air. But the tyre was nowhere. The giant vulcanized beast we'd brought to life had completely vanished; no one knew a thing about it, and being thankful and exhausted and children, we simply accepted it as a fact, and got on with the next thing.

There's probably more going on for you in the poem than there is for anyone who reads it. Your dad once made his living buying and selling tyres, so for you, those circles of carved rubber are a kind of currency or coinage. We'd be driving along some out-of-the-way road in North Yorkshire going across to the coast or up to Scotland on holiday, when he'd spy a haystack from a couple of fields away, with a sheet of black plastic over the top and half a dozen tyres holding it down. Ten minutes later you'd be sharing the back of the van with four remoulds and a pair of cross-plys, usually with water sloshing around inside them, and giving off heat like bread from the oven. Usually he'd pay for them, but there wasn't always anybody around to agree a price, so the tyres would jostle for room for the rest of the journey under an old oilcloth, like stolen sheep.

The only other time you saw your father take something that didn't belong to him was again on holiday, in Scotland, when he stopped the van at the side of a plantation of young pines, and asked your mother how much Christmas trees were going for these days. It was the middle of a very hot summer. We kept watch both ways while he pulled and wrestled with the little tree for what seemed like an hour, until the thing rocketed out of the earth and sent him spinning off into the woods. He came back covered in tiny cuts, with pine needles glued with sweat to his arms and face, and passed the mangled tree into the back of the van, still hung with a great clump of Scottish soil. When we were stopped for speeding in the Borders, you had to hold it down like a kidnapped child, and back at home he planted it in the bottom garden, away from the road, well out of sight. Pine trees mustn't travel well, or the soil wasn't right, or the shock of being attacked by your dad had finished it off. Within two weeks it was nothing but a skeleton, naked and shivering, and the rose-bay willow-herbs blew little fluffy white kisses at it from across the fence. Come Christmas, and maybe to make up for the failure, he came home with a tree that was so big it wouldn't come in through the door. Always someone to use the wrong tool if it was nearer than the right one, he went outside with a bread knife, but came back with the bottom half of the tree, having thrown the top part into the river. That year we had the only flat-topped Christmas tree in Christendom.

During the time when he was in the tyre trade, you hadn't realized how tight money must have been, until one week during the school holidays when you travelled around in the van with him. It was a bottle-green Ford Transit, with a double seat on the front passenger side, and something called a 'tickle-box' in the middle of the cabin, next to the driver's seat. What you remember about the tickle-box was that it made do as an extra seat in an emergency, and that it got very hot, especially for anyone wearing shorts who happened to brush against it with a bare leg. Its only use, as far as you could make out, was for keeping fish and chips warm on the way home. Vans don't have tickle-boxes any more – you've noticed this every time you've hired one to move house – or if they do, they've put them in the engine with all the other hot bits.

We drove around West Yorkshire for four days: Queensbury, Brighouse, Wakefield, Elland, stopping at garages and farms and mills and depots, but on Thursday night we still hadn't bought or sold a single tyre. On Friday we went further afield, places you'd never heard of and didn't recognize, out of his patch, and during the afternoon he talked less and less, and turned the radio off, and leant forward so he was almost driving with his chin on the steering wheel. Every time he stopped somewhere you'd wait in the van, watch him through the wing-mirror talking to men in brown boiler suits who were either shrugging their shoulders or shaking their heads. These silent conversations always ended with directions to another place we might try, or with a map drawn in the dust on the side of the van.

The light was going and he'd just about given up. We were driving back towards the motorway on the outskirts of Bradford, when he suddenly swung round in the middle of the road and pulled up at the top of a dirt-track running down to a dilapidated mill. He seemed to study the place for a couple of minutes, with the engine ticking over quietly, then dropped the handbrake and went bumping down the track towards the building. The inevitable Alsatian came tearing out of a half-eaten kennel, and was yanked back by a length of heavy-duty chain. Dad got out of the van and disappeared into the mill through a rolled-up metal door, and you sat there for twenty minutes, wondering how long you should wait before going inside to look for him. Suddenly he came jogging back out with a different look on his face, and drove the van around the rear of the building, into a courtyard where a man was wheeling a huge tractor tyre out of a garage, followed by another, then another, then another, until there were eight of the things leant against an old diesel tank. You hopped out and helped roll them up into the van, using two oily planks for a ramp. Before leaving, you watched him put his hand in his pocket, but the man waved him away, and half an hour later we were back at the garage in Huddersfield, with three filthy mechanics hauling the tyres out into the light, and your father doing business in the tatty little office with the blow-up Michelin Man beaming through the window. You don't know how much he got for them, but when we arrived home and he put the money in your mother's hand and folded her fingers across the wad of torn and dirty one-pound notes, she cried, and everything was good.

Maybe if he hadn't done the U-turn in the van and gone bouncing down that cinder-track, there wouldn't have been any money in the house that weekend. Maybe when he put his hand in his pocket back at the mill, there was nothing in it. Whatever the truth, he'd come home with a fortune, and after the tears had stopped we sat down in the living-room and started laughing hysterically at things that weren't even funny. It was the same day that a pole-cat had jumped out at your mother from behind the washer, so emotions were running pretty high.

The tyres were sold to exotic-sounding companies such as Honduras and Vacu-Lug, in exotic places such as Dewsbury and Keighley, to be remoulded. If they were too knackered, they went abroad, to Russia and East Germany. The remaining tread was ground off, manually, leaving a tyre 'carcass' on to which new raw-rubber treads were glued, the resin being sealed by heat in an oven as the tyre was 'cooked'. One of the reasons lorries are restricted to lower speeds is to stop a tyre becoming hot and shedding its skin. One of the reasons the hard-shoulders and central reservations of Britain's motorways are full of sloughed black hide is because wagons don't stick to the speed limit.

Tyres that were totally kaput went off to power stations to be 'crumbed' and burnt. Modern tyres won't break down in the same way because they're steel-braced, so have to be dumped in pot-holes and canyons, and burn for evermore if they catch fire, or become ecosystems for rodents and reptiles and certain plants if they don't. Dad still has theories about what to do with the world's unwanted tyres, including a plan to make a rubber path across the Pennine Way and other moorland walks, thus cutting down erosion, preventing the need to quarry expensive stone, and presumably solving the unemployment problem in the same stroke. He once went to Fort Dunlop, the Mecca of the tyre trade, on a three-week training course, and remembers that the factory was so big it had traffic lights inside the building. He also talks about one of the compounds in the tyre-making process as if it were a secret potion. Carbon Black. One teaspoon of this in its powder form, sneezed accidentally into a front-room, would coat every wall and every object in a shiny, black layer, indelibly. Those who worked in the business couldn't wash it off. It got into their skin, and under it.

When the company he worked for realized he was doing all right, they took the van off him, so he changed jobs and bought a Morris Traveller. The Morris Traveller – the only car with timbers instead of welds. When it broke down, it was better to phone for a carpenter than a mechanic. After the Morris Traveller came the Morris Minor, which eventually suffered from the same problem as every other car of its kind. One night, Christmas Day probably, we were driving home from someone else's house, the car loaded up with presents, Dad taking it slowly down the steep hill into Crimble Clough, when suddenly a car wheel went past us on the outside and rounded the bend up ahead. We watched it for five or ten mesmerizing seconds, before realizing it was the small runaway wheel of a Morris Minor, and at the moment it dawned on us, the car tipped over on to the front axle on the offside, and we came to a slow, semi-circular halt in a shower of orange sparks. Dad walked down the hill into the darkness as if he was on the trail of the tyre, tracking it down, but half an hour later he came back in a fire engine, driven by a fireman he used to work with. We went home in the cab with the big horizontal steering-wheel and the cinemascope windscreen, leaving the Morris Minor with its nose to the ground like a dog asleep on a rug, and the tyre still rolling down the valley, over the bridge and out of the universe.

You inherited a succession of your father's cars. The Austin Princess with its leatherette seats that performed skin surgery on bare flesh in hot weather. The two-litre Datsun automatic that rode up at the front when you hit the accelerator, like a speedboat. Your mother borrowed it once but couldn't find the knob to turn the cassette player down, and drove her Mothers' Union friends to a meeting in town with The Fall's *Hex Enduction Hour* in wrap-a-round stereo at full tilt on looped playback. An amber-coloured Lada, oblong like a butterscotch, that boiled over every night on the ride back from Manchester, and needed water from the horse-trough at Globe Farm before coming home through the cutting. Another Lada that made a terrifying and expensive noise when you changed gear, like stirring a bag of glass with a metal poker.

Every vehicle carried the immovable smell of pipe tobacco, no matter how many forest-fresh plastic pennants you hung on the rear-view mirror. St Bruno ready-rubbed seemed to be growing down the back of every seat and in the carpet under the rubber mats. A sack of old, rusty tools was handed down with every car, like a bag of bones.

When you left the Probation Service and cashed in your chips and counted your savings, you had just about enough for a new car. A brand new car. This was in the days when car salesmen were hanging themselves on toilet chains at the back of garages because business was so bad; if you said 'no' for long enough, they'd throw in metallic paint, a sun-roof and seven years' membership of the RAC, not to mention the number-plate and a full tank of petrol.

Part of the ritual of buying a new car is to turn up at midnight on the last day of July and drive it home through the early hours of August with all the other arseholes in their new toys. Part of the ethos of buying a new VW is to enjoy it, because if the advertising is to be believed, you'll never need to do it again. This particular year, July 31st fell on a Friday, which meant that most of the customers collecting their new Passats and Golfs and Polos and Cabriolets were half-cut in the first place, and the dealership had laid on champagne and Buck's Fizz, plus soft drinks and cheese footballs as a sop to anyone who wanted to stay on the right side of the law.

The showroom was hung with banners and streamers, and for the fifteen minutes before the appointed time, the salesmen slimed their way around the crowd, congratulating the new owners, handing over key fobs and registration documents, and raising the possibility of an extended-warranty option. You sat in one of the show cars with the doors and windows closed and the radio on. At midnight, after a final countdown and the release of hundreds of balloons from an old football net on the ceiling, the managing director of the franchise strolled out on to the balcony, took the microphone in his hand and said, 'Gentlemen, you may now go to your cars.'

It was the stuff of ceremony and sacrament, a future festival of ancient religion, the holiest day in the motorist's calendar. Bodies flooded across the forecourt, headlights blinked open and engines cleared their throats, and a convoy of L-registered Volkswagens – the people's car – turned right on to the ring road, into the witching hour.

Mum's Gone to Iceland

Water is the theme for the day. It's raining when the alarm goes off and you look out of the bedroom window, but by the time we're on the M62 the roads are drying out, and it's just coming dawn. You follow the signs through Bradford and Yeadon, overtaking the milk-floats and the first buses of the morning. When we arrive at the airport, a security guard is holding up a cardboard sign saying ICELAND, with an arrow directing us into a separate car park. Mum joins the check-in queue in the terminal, and you sidle off to the Thomas Cook's office to change fifty pounds sterling into not very many Icelandic Krona. Like all unfamiliar currency, the crisp, dry notes look like toy money, and you slip what little there is of it into your wallet. The only banknotes that actually feel like real money, you reckon, are dollars, which are nearly always dog-eared and smell of sweat – presumably the authentic odour of the American back-pocket. Mum hasn't got to the front of the line yet, so you sit to one side, watching everyone gossiping and laughing, apparently unaware that it's still only six o'clock in the morning.

When your mother asked you if you wanted to go with her on the *Yorkshire Post* readers' day trip to Iceland, your first thoughts were that you did not. You'd been to Iceland a couple of years ago and had a very trance-like and intro-spective three or four weeks, feeling you were in another life, or having one of those experiences that happens outside or parallel to everyday passages of time. To go again on a Wednesday from Leeds/Bradford airport and be back in time for a drink might somehow break the spell, or make what you'd felt before redundant, idiotic even. But when you'd checked the date of the trip and seen that it coincided with National Poetry Day, it felt like the perfect alternative to doing something embarrassing and unprofitable in the name of literature. So you'd stumped up the hundred and odd quid there and then, and put your name on the list.

You'd also thought that there might only be a handful of us, making the journey in a half-empty twin-prop commandeered for the day from an aviation museum somewhere in the region. But the concourse is packed with people, most of them retired it looks like, all of them wearing a little Monarch Airlines tag on the end of a piece of string, like a rip-cord. As well as this mark of identification, we've also been told in the itinerary to wear 'suitable clothing', and people's interpretation of this says a great deal about the Iceland they think they're visiting. 'Suitable' ranges from Gortex cagoules, North Face rucksacks and strap-on compasses, to M&S car-coats and driving gloves, to pac-a-macs and five-penny transparent rain-hoods available from all good newsagents and tobacconists. For Mr Green, a seventy- or eighty-year-old complete with name-badge presumably sewn on by an anxious relative, 'suitable' means a thick woollen suit, a thin woollen tie, a hand-knitted waistcoat and a pair of stout leather brogues. He stands next to you, rummaging in his pockets. Somebody calls his name over the tannoy, but he can't hear it because of the mounds of black, wiry hair growing out of each ear, and the Sony Walkman playing tinnitus at full volume. You picture him at the end of the day, an Icelandic flag pinned to his tie, queuing up in the duty-free with a bag of toffees and a half-bottle of Navy rum in his basket.

The theme for the day is water. The woman behind the counter in the airport café warms the teapot with hot steam before filling it and mashing the tea. She says 'Ta' instead of 'Thank you'. The five or six men in suits flying off on business trips look uncomfortable in and amongst the rabble of hikers and day-trippers, and they congregate around one table, willing their mobile phones to ring. Through the window, a heron punts across the runway and touches down on the golf-course on the other side. Sandwich boxes have already been broken into, and the whiff of potted meat kept in plastic containers begins to fill the air. Eventually we get the call, file across the Tarmac, and climb a pair of glorified step-ladders on to the plane. A woman in a knee-length quilted anorak has trouble stowing an aluminium deck-chair in the overhead locker. Mr Green is sitting in somebody else's seat. We look around for anyone we know, but surprisingly, there isn't anybody. The plane is full. The ratio of pensioners to poets is roughly three hundred and fifty to one. The temperature in Reykjavik is two degrees centigrade, and our estimated time of arrival is 9 a.m. There's an atmosphere on board like the beginning of a works outing, the sort of trip that might end in community singing and a whip-round for the driver.

There are seven tour buses ready and waiting outside Keflavik airport, one for Reykjavik only, three for the guided tour, and three for the guided tour including the Viking Lunch. Mum thought that twenty quid for a reindeer steak and baked Alaska was 'a bit on the pricey side', so we've brought sandwiches and a thermos, and we climb on to one of the coaches, pleased that about a hundred and fifty reasonable-looking people evidently thought the same thing. The first stop, on the outskirts of the capital, is a thermally heated open-air swimming baths, and we're encouraged to stand in front of a glass wall taking photographs of Icelandic citizens chugging up and down a twenty-five-metre pool. In the 'hot-pots' along the side, men and women seem to be boiling themselves in circular tubs of bubbling water, ranging from 36 to 44 degrees C, colour-coded from flesh-pink to lobster-red. You're the first back on the bus, apart from Mr Green who never got off, who snores with his head back and mouth wide open, music still leaking from his ear-plugs.

The convoy of blue coaches – fifties-looking, charabanc things – circles the city before making for the great white spire on the horizon. 'If you see a strange-looking building in Iceland, it's probably a church,' says the tour-guide. It makes a change from West Yorkshire, where if you see a church it's probably a discount carpet centre or an architect's house. We tumble off, snoop around, make a donation and climb back on board. Then it's lunchtime, and you drag Mum along to a café on the main street, where you gave a reading when you were here last time. We order coffee, and sneak sandwiches out of a bag, breaking them in half under the table.

We see a lot of each other, but you can't remember the last time you spent a whole day with your mother – just you and her. It's a thought that dawns on both of us, privately, as we sit in the window of the Café Islandus Solon in Reykjavik, Iceland, smuggling handfuls of ham roll into our mouths. The last time you had this much of her to yourself was before you started school, before she started work, and now she's retired we're picking up where we left off, with just a small matter of thirty years in between. Strangely enough, her last job was at the village infants' school, the same place she deposited the screaming cry-baby that was you at the age of three or four. You hated it: the big hall like a church with the seats taken out, the smell of sawdust, the half-pint bottles of milk warming up on the fire-escape all morning, the cloakrooms, the weird children who didn't mind being dumped in a life-size doll's house with other weird children all day – what was the matter with them? Footballs were banned from the playground, so we played with stones – you've told people this fact and they've looked sideways at you, as if you've misremembered it, which you haven't, or as if the school was some terrible, palaeolithic hell-hole, which it wasn't.

When Mum retired, they threw a bit of a party in the school, and one of the teachers took a big bunch of keys from a hook and showed me around. Music from the piano followed us up the stone staircase, like the stairwell in a tower, then past the head teacher's office with its glass front, like an old sweet shop, then into the triangular attic room with the fire-escape and windows in the ceiling. You thought you'd feel all the obvious things, about how small everything looked now and how safe and tidy. Bang your head on the beams maybe. But you could smell the sawdust, still taste the thick, warm milk at the back of your throat. You remembered the thunderstorm one afternoon when the sky was bottle green and the lights went out and we all sheltered under a desk as the lightning hunted the sky for the metal flagpole on the roof above us.

In the darkness, you looked down into the playground and told the story about the stone football, but the teacher

said, 'That doesn't sound right to me.' A cracker went off
in the hall underneath us, or a bottle of champagne. We all
ended up in one of the classrooms, sat on the tiny seats with
our knees up in front of our faces, you and your dad pour-
ing beer from the miniature plastic teapot into miniature
cups. Some of the weird children were there, thirty years
older, still looking as if everything was perfectly normal.

The tour bus makes another circuit of the city. You point
at buildings and streets from the window, saying this is
where such and such happened last time, this is where you
met so and so. Mum puts her hand over her mouth as she
yawns. Asleep, Mr Green goes past on the wrong bus in
the opposite direction. It starts to rain and the guide says,
'We have a saying in Iceland: if you don't like the weather
– wait a minute.' Half an hour later, we're travelling under
a clear blue sky along a single-track road across acres of
broken stones. The woman behind you has become
obsessed with the opening and closing of the back door
of the coach. Stopping at the sulphur pools, she leans over
to Mum, saying, 'The back door's open.' Mum nods in
agreement. 'They haven't opened it this time,' she
announces at the fish-processing plant, then, 'Open again,'
at the president's house. The president, as it happens, is
not at home, which is just as well for him because half the
party go lumbering across the lawns and gawp through
the windows. No doubt he saw the fleet of blue buses
trundling up towards him out of town, and slipped out
the back, scooting along the spit of land in his Nissan
Micra, making for the interior.

The last stop of the day, and also the highlight of the trip
for which we've forked out an extra fiver, is the Blue

Lagoon. As the bus climbs over the last volcanic hill, we see the lagoon about a mile in front of us, a cloud of steam rising from the green, opalescent water. On its own it would be a miracle, an oasis of colour in a landscape of inert, grey stones. But the massive power-plant behind it somehow deadens the effect, especially when we hear that the efficacious water we're about to immerse ourselves in is a by-product from a heat-transfer process. The guide explains that the naturally hot water from under the earth is 'too much in clogging and clagging' to be put through pipes, so it's used to heat surface water, then drained into a pond. When changing huts are erected around the pond, it becomes a pool, and when the rich minerals of the earth's interior are added into the equation, it becomes a spa.

You strip off in one of the cubicles and follow the slotted wooden walkway outside. There are a couple of seconds in which you're conscious of standing in the open air in a freezing wind in a pair of trunks in front of a power station in Iceland, and then the warmth from the pool drifts up the gang-plank towards you, and you take the plunge.

It's very, very hot. You swim out to the middle, and tread water with half a dozen people from the bus. Mum's face looks the way it does when she cooks Christmas dinner – red cheeks, hair wet with steam. Mr Green sits on one of the salt-coloured islands like a cormorant on a rock. Those who didn't bring a swimming costume watch from the pier, stamping their feet to keep warm. Those of us in the water breathe the magic vapour to the bottom of our lungs, feel the precious crystals between our toes, let the electric-blue elixir draw the aches and pains from swellings and creaky joints, and loll about like seals after feeding time, contemplating eternal life.

*

It's just gone eleven when we land back in Yorkshire. There's a hold-up on the runway, then we have to queue outside the building in a light drizzle before passing through passport control, then have to queue again at the customs desk. Mum gets irritated with the wait, and says something, and the woman in front in a green headscarf turns round and says, 'Better safe than sorry.'

'I suppose so.'

A couple of minutes later, a man with a pale white face, carrying his glasses in his hands, walks towards the woman in the headscarf and puts his arm around her shoulder.

'Gary, what are you doing here?'

'Mary, you'd better come with me. Come on, love.'

She lets out a little giggle of surprise, but when she sees that he isn't laughing, she looks up at him for some kind of explanation.

'What is it?'

'Come on, Mary, love.'

He guides her to a door at the side of the concourse, and pushes it open. Inside the small room, two younger women move forward to comfort her, and behind them a policeman, and behind the policeman, a priest. The door closes. The queue moves slowly forward, and as we pass the room, we hear the sound of crying.

Lighting-Up Time

I preached near Huddersfield to the wildest congregation
I have seen in Yorkshire, yet they were restrained by an
unseen hand.
– John Wesley's Journal, 1759

Christmas Eve, you walk down to the Christingle service in
the village with your mother, and Laurie your niece and
Jonathan your nephew. Christingle is a junior version of
Midnight Mass, introduced to discharge some of the static
electricity that most children are primed with at this time
of year, and to try to connect Christmas with the Church.
Tonight, St Bartholomew's has a full house, side to side and
front to back, but apparently it isn't as full as in years gone
by, when the kids ran riot and the vicar smiled, holding a
painted melon above his head, announcing the birth of Jesus.

There's a brief sermon on the Germanic origins of the
service, delivered from behind a lectern in the shape of a
soaring eagle, giving the vicar the look of an aerobatics
stunt-man lashed above the wings of a single-seater plane.
Lots of crying and screaming and looking for lost children
under pews and behind curtains. A long queue for the one
toilet in the vestry. The church like an aviary, full of strange
sounds and exotic noises flitting from one wooden beam
to another up under the roof.

The high point is the distribution of the Christingles,
in which all the children (and some of the excitable adults)
surge forward to collect what looks like a First-World-War

hand-grenade – an orange with a candle jammed in its navel, stabbed by four cocktail sticks, each sporting a jelly tot or a sultana. Every orange is finished off with a red ribbon around its equator. The vicar reminds us that we hold in our hands the fruit of the earth and the light of the world, and the four seasons and the bread of heaven, and the death, and the resurrection. After receiving their payload, the children perform an orderly procession along the outside aisles and back up the middle, until gridlock occurs. Then all candles are lit, the next from the last, and the house lights are cut. Each child stands with a face like a mask, lit from below. *Away in a Manger* is sung, and you amaze yourself by remembering most of the words, and flush out a couple of tears from each eye by blinking, and take them into your mouth with the tip of your tongue.

The vicar makes his closing remarks, including some safety tips on the extinguishing of the candles. When the lights go on, most of the jelly tots have disappeared, and three eight-year-olds have set fire to the cocktail sticks and are dangling the red ribbons in the flames. A parent steps in as an arson attack on the Lady Chapel looks possible. Another boy drips molten wax into the hood of his brother's anorak, and a little girl spears herself in the nostril while attempting to eat one of the sweets from the wooden skewer. The church is hazy with blue smoke, as if some ancient ritual or powerful act of magic had taken place, involving sacrifice and fire.

The big doors open on to a cold, clear night. Parents lead their families along the churchyard and through the iron gates at the far end, towards Christmas Day morning. Your mother and the children climb into a car and turn the corner. Half a dozen of you stand in the doorway, not in any rush to go anywhere, see anyone.

Under the stars, someone notices the sky, and points out the constellations with the burning, laser-red tip of a cigarette. Aries, grazing in the path of the planets. Orion the hunter, with one foot in the river, lifting his club and his shield to the great orange eye of Taurus the bull. Pegasus, the winged horse, with the fish of Pisces splashing about under its hooves and Andromeda reaching out for its reins. The flickering silver pulse of Sirius just above the horizon – a filling in the mouth of the great dog Canis, baring its teeth at Lepus the hare. Ursa Major and Ursa Minor, the great bear and its cousin, tethered to Polaris, plodding eternally like circus animals around the North Star. And Gemini, the twins, falling through space together at arm's length, repelled and obsessed at the same time, pushing each other away and hanging on for grim death. Your stars. Your sign.

The cigarette gets flicked away, upwards into the bare branches of trees lining the graveyard, into the Milky Way. Then you split up, go your separate ways, towards different lives under the same patch of the sky.

POCKET PENGUINS

POCKET PENGUINS